A MYRIAD OF ROADS THAT LEAD TO HERE

NATHAN ELIAS

Scarlet Leaf

2017

ISBN: 978-1975786366

PUBLISHED BY SCARLET LEAF

Toronto, Canada

for my mother

who left too soon

"With each breath, we fade far from each other, the sky's weight pressing on us. We push back for we must be more than ideas or we'll die."

Rane Arroyo, The Sky's Weight

A Myriad of Roads That Lead to Here

I've just hitched my first ride and I'm sitting in the back of a flatbed truck called Wild Child across from my friend Saul, and I feel bad for him because he's balding and can't feel his hair whip around his face like I can. I force my eyes wide open to take in the world for what it is—a blur of countryside and mountains, lush greens and ash greys whizzing past me as I barrel down Route 208 just outside of Grove City, Pennsylvania, heading east. I nudge Saul and point to the sky, a spiral of oranges, blues, and pinks, but he's too busy gripping the steel siding of the flatbed to look up. I should probably be holding on for dear life like he is, but for a moment I tell myself I might find some peace right now if I just let go for a little while longer.

Wild Child drops us off fifteen miles away from Shipperville, where we were trying to arrive before nightfall, but here on a tall hillside the light has already begun its descent. Here it is, our first night on our trip, 230 miles away from Toledo, and we're about to be forced into our red child-sized tent, which I bought under the impression it would be lighter in the long run. We set up in a grassy field clearly on someone's property, their house not twenty yards up the hill.

"I don't know, West," Saul says. "People in these kinds of places probably have shotguns. We shouldn't just sleep on someone's property."

"What other choice do we have?" I ask. I know he agrees because he doesn't argue. I tell him all we can do it set up and try to play it cool and be respectable to the land, and if anyone gives us trouble that we just get up and leave nice and politely. For the fifty-something hours we spent planning and discussing what it would be like sleeping outside, we always assumed that we would be immersed in nature the entire time—but this is anything but. It takes us about forty minutes to set up the tent in the dark, and once we're set up we eat granola bars and jerky, which is already running low. We discuss the day—the forty miles of walking before finally hitching a ride with Wild Child, how we never planned on hitchhiking rides but now it seemed like a good idea. We agree that we severely miscalculated how to pack. The weight of our packs is seventy-two pounds each, over our maximum capacity. Our packs contain: two changes of clothes, the child-sized tent, one sleeping bag each, two knives, rice, oatmeal, granola bars, jerky, a compass, two maps of Pennsylvania, *Leaves of Grass*, *Walden*, *The Teachings of the Buddha*, *A Buddhist Bible*, and three notebooks which I carry myself.

"Can we just leave the books?" Saul asks.

"We're not leaving the books. If we leave the books, the whole trip will seem trivial."

"We're not aesthetic pilgrims, West." He drops his books in the dirt.

"Aren't we looking for truth? Enlightenment? Transcendence? Whatever it is that will cleanse us both of the distress we feel from losing our mothers?"

Saul picks up his books, wipes off the dirt, and returns them to his bag.

His mother died when he was eleven. His oldest brother, Mike, found her after she slipped in the shower. I never knew this about Saul but he told me everything when my mom died in June. We were both pretty wasted, and even though I knew that his mother had died, it was like for the first time he had someone to share his pain with other than his brothers.

We chalk it up to poor planning and Saul convinces me that hitching rides won't be any less admirable or adventurous than walking straight to the ocean. About a month after Mom passed I was sitting under the stars with Lena, I had just asked her to be official with me. We were on the High-Level Bridge, and I had been telling myself for months to be single, to not fall in love again, to find myself—but she was there for me when I was broken, so I gave in. I had the realization, with her in my arms, believing that I could be the one for her, and myself trying to convince myself the same, when I realized that I had to get away from Toledo and all the friends I knew and all the women I loved and all the ghosts that found their way into my heart. It was the middle of summer, all of which I had spent working at Barnes and Noble and cleaning a Lutheran church, and writing articles for free for the college independent paper. The first year of college I chose to read books like *Walden* and research Buddhism on my own time, and really started to believe that something was out there to be discovered that could wash the pain from me and anyone else who chose to search for it and see it truly.

I curl up in my sleeping bag and hear Saul drift away to sleep. I wish I wasn't consumed by fear and could convince my body to get some rest, but I unzip the tent's flap and step outside. With my bare feet in the grass, I flick my lighter and inhale from one of my emergency cigarettes. The stars tonight in Pennsylvania look the same to me as they did that night with Lena when I thought up the idea to take this trip, to hike to the ocean and back, all before school started at the end of the month. I drag the cigarette half way down, focusing on the orange end, and look to the five scars on my left bicep, gleaming in the moonlight. I breathe deep, and remind myself to be in the present moment, to not dwell in the past. I look up at the small house on the hillside and there is a single window illuminated. Inside someone stands there, looking out at me, smoking their own cigarette.

We wake up just before the sun rises, reorganize our packs, disassemble the tent, and continue east. The hills seem to go on forever, and the road continues stretching further than our eyes can see. There are no cars for the first two hours of our walk. Even if Saul wasn't the quiet type, we wouldn't be speaking because our bodies are at maximum workload as it is. We stop at a clearing overlooking the first downward hill in miles. Saul opens a can of refried beans. There's a thick chunk of bacon resting atop the beans.

"You want to split that?"

"All yours," I say. Saul reaches his fingers into the can and devours the fatty pork, chewing it like a hungry dog. I dig through my pack for plastic spoons, pass one to Saul, and take a mouthful of sweet, savory beans. Once I feel the protein pumping through my veins I'm ready to walk again.

Throughout the course of the day we hitch a total of three rides, taking us thirty miles through Clintonville to Clarion. Around three o'clock we're surrounded by commerce and highways intersecting, the kind of place that is hard to score a ride because everyone is in a rush. I decide to get us a room at the Motel 6 with my credit card. I find it hard to believe that I can continue walking without a proper shower or bed. Saul doesn't openly complain about the pain he's experiencing but he doesn't hesitate when I pay for the room, either.

Saul has no money, and part of our arrangement was that I would pay for everything and that whatever we spent he would later pay for half. I know this will never happen because Saul has never had a job, but I needed someone to come with me and he was the only one willing. In honesty, I don't know if there is another friend I'd rather have with me. I've learned that it's hard to relate to people who haven't had their hearts ripped out of them.

Once we're in the room Saul turns the air conditioner up all the way, jumps in the bed, and clicks on the television. He kicks his boots to the floor. Blood seeps through his dirty sock.

"I knew I should have cut my toenails before we left," he says and winces in pain while removing the bloody sock before tossing it onto the air conditioner.

I nearly gag but choose to ignore Saul's gross gesture. I take the map from my pack and spread it across the other double bed.

"Originally, we planned to hike through the Allegheny Forest, over the Appalachian Mountains, into New York City, and finally get to the ocean in Jersey. I figured we would rest for a few days and then turn back."

Saul cracks a laugh at something happening on the TV. It occurs to me that Saul couldn't care less about the trip. Maybe he just has complete faith in me, I think.

"This trip could kill us," I say. "What were we thinking?"

"We? This was your harebrained idea." Saul suddenly gets hysterical over the television show.

"You know, I spent the past weeks researching maps and nature books of Pennsylvania while I stood for countless hours at the Barnes and Noble cash registers, which were conveniently located by the travel section."

"Looking at maps doesn't make you an explorer, West."

For some reason, I start cracking up with him and the laugh track, even though I know I'm really laughing at myself.

"Saul, I'm sorry for getting us into this mess."

"Are you apologizing to me or to yourself?" I don't know how to answer his question. He sees that I'm stunned and turns the TV off. "You've got to look at the bright side, man. We're out here. We're doing it."

"We're staying at a hotel but we're supposed to be roughing it."

"We should press on and not give up. Never give up. Even if we have to change our plans a little. My brother lives in Harrisburg. We could stay with him for a couple days."

I start to think of my own family in Dunbar, distant cousins on my father's side who I have only seen a few times in my life.

"Sure," I say. "Give him a call."

"Alright, then." Saul picks up the hotel phone and calls his brother. I step out to call Lena on my cell. The parking lot sits on the edge of a hill looking over the top of a field of trees.

"Weston!" Lena answers when I call, her voice high-pitched, excited to hear mine. We're still at the stage where we haven't said 'I love you'. We haven't been physical other than kissing. "It feels like you've already been away for months. I miss you so much."

"I'm thinking about you," I lie. In truth, my body has been so sore that I haven't thought about anything but the pain and the road. But I know enough about her fragile, virgin feelings to keep up appearances. "Will you send me some pictures?" I try to make my voice sound seductive. I really just want to see her naked.

I go back inside once the sun sets and send her a picture of me to get her going. Saul just shakes his head.

"My brother will let us stay but he's kind of pissed about the whole thing. I should have given him more notice."

"Look Saul, I don't think it's a good idea. I'm trying to dodge negative energy." But Saul assures me that his brother is always like this because he's resistant to change, but that he's a good-hearted guy once you get to know him.

*

The next morning, we check out and get an early start on the road. We get three rides that take us sixty miles from Clarion to Clearfield and get another hotel for the night. The day has blessed us with down-to-earth people and good weather. After miles in the sunlight what can only be Murphy's Law kicks in—dark, smoky-looking clouds loom over the horizon. They promise thunderstorms by tomorrow.

*

We fill up on continental breakfast the next morning and begin again. It feels good to have a destination. We plan for Harrisburg by the end of the week, and hope to pass State College and Lewiston by the end of the day. The road and the people of Pennsylvania are kind to us. An old woman gives me a twenty without explanation other than a smile. A young girl in State College picks us up and says that seeing us inspires her, and reminds her of her favorite book.

"*On the Road* by Jack Kerouac," she says.

"I've never read that one," I say.

"For guys like you, I'd say it's necessary." Her smile is bright, wide, and reminds me of Lena.

The Appalachian Mountains come into view and tower over us. We pass their walls without fault or trouble until we reach the other side. Outside Lewiston the sky promises rain. Hours pass on the side of the highway. The air thickens, but we are saved by an elderly guy in a rickety van.

"My wife died of breast cancer," he tells us an hour into the trip, after the pleasantries. He's already offered to take us all the way to Harrisburg. "She would stay up to watch Phillies baseball games even though I thought they were boring. She used to say, 'Phillies games make time stand still and make me feel like I'll live forever.'"

He drops us off in Harrisburg and I can't thank him enough for driving us the sixty miles, and I am moved to tears by his pain and honesty.

Saul uses my cell phone to call his brother, and we wait for him for about forty-five minutes in the parking lot of an old run down grocery store.

"You're soaking wet," he says. He looks a lot like Saul but balder and about one hundred pounds over Saul's one-forty. "You're going to drench the interior of my new car, but it's really no big deal."

I feel like crap climbing into the backseat of the car, now. Thankfully, Saul is up front this time otherwise I'd have an anxiety attack.

"So how has your little expedition been?" Mike asks. "Living up to your expectations?"

"Pretty good so far," Saul answers. "Met a lot of interesting people."

"Both of you need to be careful. It's crazy, what you're doing. Real crazy."

I don't like being called crazy, so I try to focus on incoming texts from Lena.

The first text is a picture of her in a sports bra and white cotton panties, lying on her stomach so that I can only see the gentle curves of her body. It's still enough to give me an erection that I must now try to hide.

After the picture, she sends a message that reads, All urs when u get back. XoXo <3

The last thing I need is to be distracted by sex. I turn my phone off and try to fix my gaze again upon the world. Mike's eyes catch mine from his rear-view mirror.

"So how does Pennsylvania compare to Ohio?"

"The buildings here are decrepit and remind me of how rundown Toledo is," I say. "So far Pennsylvania has been beautiful—landscape, nature, and hills. But Harrisburg is the first sign of a city that resembles Toledo. I can't figure out which one is worse or more depressing."

"Maybe that's why I like it here," Mike says. "It's like being back home without being there."

*

Once we get to Mike's apartment, his wife, Sharon, holds the door for us with her baby, Melissa, in tow. Immediately I feel like I'm intruding on these people's lives and decide that we can't stay for long. I make note to tell this to Saul later when we're alone.

Mike and Sharon order pizza to go with the twenty-four pack of beer they got to welcome us with.

"Saul told us about your mother," Mike says. He bites into the largest slice of pepperoni pizza from the box.

"We're both so sorry for your loss," Sharon says.

"Yes," Mike continues, "we're both really sorry."

"Thank you. That means a lot." I realize that I shouldn't feel like I'm putting them out, that they're opening their heart and homes to have us and welcome me as part of their family.

I come to learn that Sharon is a nurse, and of course as soon as she gets a look at the scars on my bicep she asks how I got them.

"Isn't that a little personal, honey?" Mike asks. His cheeks go red.

"It's okay," I say before the poor guy can get too embarrassed. I stick out my bicep like it's being examined under a microscope. "I'm used to it. I put them there with my dad's fishing knife when I found Corinne, my girlfriend of a year and a half at the time and with a history of cutting, sitting cross-legged on my bedroom floor doing the same to her inner thighs."

This conversation never bodes well with people, but I figure it's the truth and if they're going to ask I might as well tell it.

"There are all kinds of different ways you could mend the scars and reduce their visibility with certain lotions and ointments," Sharon tells me. I write them all down in my journal, but I never actually plan to apply this information. I know she means well, but I don't know if there is really a point in trying to erase the scars.

Mike and Sharon go to bed and leave the rest of the beer to Saul and me. We down every bottle, happy to be resting in a nice place without having to pay for it. Outside the apartment window is a sign made of giant, red luminous letters that spell CLEANER, for the cleaning service below. I open the window and step out to the awning under the bright letters, take a picture of myself, and send it to Lena. Saul follows me out, closing the window behind him.

"Earlier when you were in the shower Mike and Sharon offered to drive us to Ocean City and back," Saul says. "How would you feel about that?"

"Taking a ride the whole way would destroy the spirit of the trip," I say.

"You're wrong. It's only a four-hour drive one way. They would love to take a day trip out to the ocean with Melissa anyway."

"Can I sleep on it?"

"It doesn't always have to be difficult, West. It doesn't always have to be life or death."

I stand outside and smoke a cigarette while Saul falls asleep with old reruns on again. I go inside and I lay awake staring at the walls, changing color from the glow of the TV. As much as I feel that taking the ride to the ocean will make me feel bent to Mike's will, I also figure that I can't keep putting motel rooms on my credit card because it's already nearly maxed out. I close my eyes and fall asleep on the floor inside my sleeping bag.

*

Before getting on the expressway for New Jersey we stop at the dollar store to buy sandals for Saul and myself, as well as other miscellaneous travel items we need for the trip and possibly the ocean. I haven't told Saul, yet, but I plan on getting to the ocean and staying there, letting Mike, Sharon, and Melissa return to Harrisburg without us. I tell myself that their ride will not be in vain and that we could potentially go see New York still, like we planned.

Saul and I sit in the backseat with Melissa between us. She sleeps and keeps quiet for most of the trip, only crying a few times. Her cries do not bother me and in fact remind me of how I am really feeling inside, wishing I could cry, wishing that my mother were sitting in the front seat, within arm's reach, every so often checking on me to give me a smile, to realign me to a peaceful state.

"You're a good mom, Sharon," Saul says. He stares out the window without looking at her.

"Thank you, Saul. That means a lot." Melissa coos.

Saul doesn't answer. I wonder if he's trying to hold back tears.

*

For most of the four hours I write in my journal about things I haven't had time to think of: what my life will be like without my mother, the fact that I may actually be in severe credit card debt after this trip, whether all of it is worth it, and what I plan to do when I get back. I write out in great detail what I need to do to complete all of my unfinished projects—the music documentary I've been working on for two years now, and the novel that was all about how I, the protagonist, take a long-awaited trip to see my family in Dunbar. I decide that when we get back to Harrisburg I will call my cousin, Maggie, and ask if Saul and I can stay for a short time.

When we park at the beach in Ocean City, all of the blue has been sucked from the sky so it and the sea are a vast canvas of hazy gray. It is not the amalgamation of warmth and color I pictured. There are hardly any people out swimming due to the rain.

"I've come too far to not wade into the ocean," I say, taking my shirt off before I head into the water.

"Come on, nobody's going in the water," Mike says, pointing wildly at everyone on the beach.

"It's far too cold," Sharon cries. "If you go in you're at risk of pneumonia."

To my surprise, Saul is right behind me ready to wade in. We step out and a small wave catches our legs. The water is like icy knives against my flesh. We continue in and dive under, splashing around.

"Pretty cold," Saul says. His teeth chatter.

"It's cold in a liberating way, though," I say.

"I can't take it anymore." Saul heads toward the shore.

I can barely move my limbs so I figure I should follow him before I drown in the gray, glistening water.

Mike watches us walk back from the waves, shaking his head. "Great. Now I'm going to have to clean all of this sand out of the car." Nobody says anything. Not Sharon, not Saul, not me, not the baby. Mike clears his throat. "What do you say we get heading back?"

"Heading back?" I ask. I can't keep my mouth shut any more. "We wanted to go to New York."

"There's no way you could cross to New York without a car," Sharon says.

"Look," Mike says, taking the baby, "we didn't plan on taking you that far. Besides, there is no guarantee you'll be able to hitch a ride."

"Okay, well maybe we can head to Boston," I suggest.

"It's really not going to be any easier," Mike says.

"What if we reroute to the Allegheny Forest?"

"Then at least come back with us," Sharon says. "Please."

"Okay, let's find a middle ground," Saul says. He puts his arms up like a crossing guard. "Can we just stay for a few more hours and walk along the boardwalk? After that we can drive back to Harrisburg and figure it out from there."

I can't admit defeat. I can't verbally admit to leaving the place I dreamed of reaching, so I stare at the ground and try to take in the landscape and the people and we walk along the boardwalk until the sun sets. I make sure to take everything in—the surfboards and the beach houses and Atlantic City's bustle echoing off the distant shore.

"I hate to cut this short but we have to get the baby back," Mike says. Saul and I pile into the back seat. He gives me a look and shrugs his shoulders.

"Look, I'm sorry," Saul says. "I know how much it means to you. It's better this way. We're still having an adventure."

"It's just not the same," I say.

"Four hours to Harrisburg," Mike says once he's in the car. "Better pee now if you have to go because we ain't stopping."

*

I'm trapped in Harrisburg, I think all night. I can't escape the rage I feel from Mike and Sharon's attempt at kindness, which actually made the trip all the worse. I argue with myself, tossing and turning until five in the morning. Everyone else is fast asleep.

Before anyone wakes up I sneak back out the window and call Maggie.

"Of course, I'd love to have you and Saul," she says. "I didn't even know you were in Pennsylvania. I'd be offended if you didn't come see us. You know we miss you, kid. Just call me when you're close."

I go back inside and read *Walden* until Sharon and the baby wake up. She starts a breakfast of bacon, eggs, and toast. While she beats the eggs I look across the table into Melissa's cradle. She looks into my eyes, unblinking, and smiles wide. Saul and Mike wake when the bacon starts to sizzle and before I know it the peace and quiet have evaporated.

"I'm sorry for arguing with you guys when you tried to stay in Ocean City," Sharon says. "It really wasn't my place, but I kept picturing something awful happening to the two of you. If something did happen I wouldn't be able to live with myself."

"Don't worry about it," I say with a piece of bacon in my mouth, grinding the fat with my teeth.

I'm feeling more excited about seeing my own family again and give the news to Saul after breakfast.

"I want to leave today," I tell him. "I want to get a move on."

"I was thinking we could stay for a few more days," he says. I can tell I've thrown him for a loop. Sharon picks up the baby and leaves the room with Mike for Saul and I to discuss the matter.

"I'm starting to worry about finances and getting back in time for school," I tell him. "It wouldn't be fair if I can't spend much time with my family. You can't really argue me on this one."

"And why can't I argue you?" he asks. "If it weren't for me you'd be alone on this trip."

"I've paid for everything so far."

He doesn't respond. He knows I'm right.

"While you were asleep I planned a route for us to take to Dunbar," I say. "We've gotten approximately eleven rides so far, averaging four rides a day. We can't know if we will get any rides so we have to estimate for the maximum amount of time."

"Can I have a minute to explain this to my brother and sister-in-law?" he asks. "I'm afraid us hitchhiking is going to give them a panic attack, but maybe they can drop us off near the expressway."

After Saul comes out of Sharon and Mike's room I watch him try to hide while drying tears from his eyes. I feel like shit for creating this negative energy between him and his family.

"Alright, Mike says he'll take us in twenty minutes," Saul says.

I nod and turn toward my scattered gear when Sharon swings the bedroom door open. I hear crying which I assume is the baby in her arms, but it's actually Sharon.

"Come here, Saul," she says, holding her brother-in-law with one arm while she kisses his cheek. "You too, Weston." I walk over to them and let her embrace me. I embrace back.

"We're giving you money and food to take with you," Sharon says.

"We are?" Mike asks from the bedroom doorframe.

"Yes, we are. Give them a hundred bucks and all the dried fruit, nuts, and granola we have in the apartment."

"Really, you don't have—" I start to say.

"I insist," Sharon growls. There's no way I could argue that, so I just stand aside and pack while Mike fumbles for the cash and the food.

*

When Mike drops us off he gives Saul a giant pat on the back. I envisioned them hugging, but I guess that's not the kind of thing they do.

"Well, I wish you both good luck," Mike says. "Maybe Sharon, the baby, and I will come visit Toledo for Thanksgiving."

"That'd be cool, Mike," Saul says. He repetitiously rubs his palm against his balding head.

"Thanks for everything, Mike," I say. "It really means a lot. It was great to meet you. Your brother is a good friend."

"He's a good brother, too," Mike says.

We get out of the car and watch Mike drive off down the highway until his car is out of view. When I turn back toward the on-ramp with my thumb stretched out, I see a single tear run from Saul's eye.

"What's wrong?" I ask.

He sniffles and turns the other way.

"He called me a good brother," he says, stretching his thumb toward oncoming traffic.

We walk for hours, barricaded by the highway infrastructure, unable to get a ride. During our rides, we have seldom had to walk along the expressway—mostly just sticking to scenic state routes. It proves impossible to escape. I wonder if there is some bad karmic energy prohibiting us from hitching a ride.

After ditching the expressway, we wander the streets of downtown Harrisburg looking for a place to loiter, catch our breaths, regroup. There are no restaurants, no diners, no coffee shops or stores. There is a hospital, and at this hour the emergency room is open.

"Maybe we should call my brother and ask if we can stay for another night."

"I couldn't stand bothering your uptight brother anymore. We ought to take a bus."

"We don't have anywhere to sleep tonight."

"Let's just go into the emergency room so we can at least sit down. I'm afraid of street vagrants. Can we please sit down and try to figure out some kind of plan?"

He obliges so we enter through the automatic doors of the emergency room. I tell him to follow my lead, and I act as if I'm looking for someone. The waiting room is practically full. I know how these places work because I've been in them multiple times with no explanation, getting calls from my stepfather that my mother admitted herself again. When I'd arrive, I would know exactly where to go beforehand and was never stopped once. This time is no different. We sit and blend in with the rest of the people. Saul is uneasy; he says that we stick out with our large backpacks. Everyone stares at us. I tell Saul not to worry, that people will assume one of us is injured and waiting, or we are waiting for a friend who is inside. We sit in the waiting room for two hours. I try to text Lena but there is no answer, this one time when I need her most. She must be away or watching her nephew, but I don't let Saul know that inside I'm feeling fractured because we have no place to go and I can't bring myself to let him ask his brother. I wish I could swallow my pride; for him and I to hang tight in the waiting room feels too privileged. Some people around us are truly injured, some bleeding, some crying or trying to withhold their screams, some loved ones cradling others, whispering that everything will be alright, saying their prayers to God aloud.

Lena finally calls me and when I answer she apologizes a hundred times. I tell her that it's okay because I don't need apologies, what I need is someone who has Google. I step outside to the smoking area and light one of my emergency cigarettes while Lena searches some hotels in the area. We figure prices for the better part of an hour. I ask her to look up if there are any trains or buses leaving soon that head west. She finds a bus that leaves tomorrow morning at eleven heading for Johnstown for eighty dollars per ticket. So, we have a way out of Harrisburg but we still don't have a way out of the night. I ask Lena to look up if there are any men's shelters nearby, and after a few minutes of her typing she tells me that there is a place called Bethesda Mission three miles from our current location. She quotes from their site, "Dedicated to providing hope and healing to the homeless and hurt people of the Greater Harrisburg Area."

Saul and I leave the hospital and return to the dark streets, eyeballed by nightwalkers and beggars. For the entirety of the walk to the Bethesda Mission we keep our pocketknives close at hand, afraid of getting mugged or worse. When we round the corner onto Basin Street, we see the big green cross with "Bethesda Mission" in white. On the staircase leading up to the four giant, white pillars, haggard men look at us like we're fresh meat. We pass the pillars and enter the large wooden doors into the red brick building. A man at a desk welcomes us, answers our questions about staying, and says that he can get us a bed for the night. We produce our identification and fill out the necessary paperwork.

The man at the desk tells us that the night is wrapping up and guides us to a gymnasium with a stage and rows of metal chairs lined up in front of it. There is a man below the stage standing behind a podium reading from the bible. We sit in one of the empty rows and listen in for the rest of the sermon, praying when the haggard men pray and joining in with them when they sing. After two hours and bathing in the community showers, all of the men create a work line to remove mattresses and blankets from a storage locker, line them all down in the gymnasium where the metal chairs once were, and finally lie down to wait for lights out. I fall asleep faster than I thought.

*

The man from the desk turns the lights back on at five in the morning, and the men routinely return the beds and blankets to the storage locker.

My eyes snap open to the bright fluorescent lights and at first I can't remember where I am. As men around me rise from the linoleum auditorium floors like zombies from a graveyard, I remember instantly.

Next to me Saul is still snoring, oblivious to the worker blaring a foghorn to force everyone from their hopeful slumber.

"Time to get up," I mutter with a hoarse voice. He doesn't respond so I nudge him with my foot until he jolts awake, gasping for air.

"I dreamt that you drowned in the Allegheny River," Saul says. "I couldn't save you. I couldn't save myself."

"Well, I'm not drowned," I say. "We have to help put the beds and blankets back." The thought of drowning makes nausea rise up from my stomach to my head. Saul looks around at the men lined up for the storage locker.

"This place ain't so bad," he says. "There's more order in here than there is out there."

"What do you mean?"

"I don't see anybody drowning. Do you?" Half of the men have their eyes closed still while they drag the heavy mattresses across the smooth floor.

*

Once we're back on the streets of downtown Harrisburg I turn to Saul and notice that his eyes are practically glued to the pavement.

"Cheer up, Saul. This is the makings of the universe and proof that things are interconnected."

"I'm sorry but it's not always easy for me to see everything as beautiful, like you."

"Take the last few days, for example. Look at how many strangers have been kind to us. Don't you think the cosmos has something to do with it all?"

He slants his head, stopping in his tracks. His silence is answer enough.

"Got it," I say. "I'll shut up for a while."

*

When we arrive at the bus station the first thing I notice are the tall, glossy oak hallways. The inside of the bus station here is so picturesque that it almost makes up for the musty smell that I inhale like a thick fume. It's dark with small families, some with children, waiting for a train or bus. There are a few homeless people sleeping on the benches and the station guards don't seem to have a problem with them, but I can't remember seeing any homeless people like this in Toledo. Even around the Cherry Street Mission people didn't sleep out on benches or at the Greyhound station.

The area where we wait for our bus is outside the station in a smaller, white linoleum area. As Saul reads *Walden* I try to calculate my finances but cannot focus. There are bubblegum machines with candy I haven't seen in years, the kind where you put in a quarter, twist the metal knob, and candy pours into your hand. I spend fifty cents on the candy and notice a little Latino boy staring at me as I eat it. His mother is arguing with the old man at the ticket booth. I walk by the boy, making it look like I'm passing him for the phone booth, and set fifty cents on the table next to him. He smiles and goes to buy himself two handfuls of candy.

I step outside because after a few passive quarrels with Saul, I'd really like to talk to someone I know will be on my side no matter what. I step outside and dial Lena, resting near the shade of a pine tree.

"Are you okay?" she asks. "Did you make it to the station?"

"We're at the station. We got the tickets and are set to leave for Johnstown in an hour and a half."

"How was the homeless shelter? Was it scary? Did anybody mess with you?"

"It actually wasn't that bad. We all slept on mattresses in an auditorium."

"I wish you would have just let me loan you money for a hotel."

"Taking money from loved ones isn't in the nature of the trip. The entire purpose is to find freedom. Independence. How can I ever expect to find freedom and independence if I keep depending on people?"

"Weston, you look at dependence like it is weak. It's not weak. It's okay to let other people love you. You know that, right?"

At first, I don't know what to say. I open my mouth and attempt to formulate words but, actually, no, I think. I didn't really know that. Is this Lena's way of trying to tell me she loves me for the first time?

"I've got to get going," I say. "But thank you for everything, Lena. I'll text you when we get on the bus."

She exhales slowly. I can only hope she isn't crying.

When I get back inside I see the Latino boy's mother asking him where he got the candy, and the boy is pointing at Saul who swears he didn't give it to the kid. I go up to the boy's mother and tell her the whole thing and apologize, and for the rest of the wait she stares at me with her eyebrows cocked.

The bus arrives and there is enough space for us both to take our own rows in the back and stretch out.

"I should have brought my guitar," Saul says. "Maybe when we get back you can buy one and I'll teach you how to play. We can start a band."

"You know I'm learning piano," I say.

"I've heard you play. You'd need to get a lot better before you could play in my band."

*

The bus ride lasts four hours with a rest stop half way. When we arrive in Johnstown we exit the bus to find the city as one big enclave, mountains on all sides. It takes a minute to find our bearings so we walk up and down various boulevards trying to gauge a safe path for us to trek. I always fear pulling out the map and looking lost, vulnerable to any crazies who may be lurking. We ask a few locals which main road would be good to walk down, and they guide us toward Franklin, so we walk southwest down the long road, all the buildings tan and red brick, some modernized with wide glass panes. There is a McDonald's where we rest, eat, pull out the map, and figure that we can begin our quest to Dunbar by taking route 271 which winds south and comes back north before its straight path west. It's the quickest route we can find even with that small amount of backtracking.

Franklin Avenue takes us past the Johnstown commerce, small thrift shops, a Salvation Army, and even an outdoor art show with local artists selling their watercolor replicas of the lush trees encircling their city. As we cross the towering steel bridge I look over the side to see the slow rapids of the Conemaugh River below. It's easy to confuse the water below with the robin's egg blue of the bridge's surface. We continue down Franklin until we reach 271 at Menoher Boulevard where the ramshackle boxed houses, tans and reds and blues and greens line the hillside, cascading upward where our trail leads us. We pass the houses and there is only the narrow road and the trees. We cling to the shoulder with our thumbs stretched for two hours along the winding road, sandwiched between vehicles careening around sharp turns and the exposed rock wall on our right. Saul says that he's been feeling sick and needs to rest. I don't want to admit it, but so do I. The heat from the sun grips us. The uphill hike teaches us the strength of gravity—I'm surprised we haven't passed out yet. We find shade near a building that looks brand new. We can't figure out if it's a church or a school, but there is a pool in the back and we smell barbecue. Under the shade, I try to convince Saul that we could go back behind the building and introduce ourselves and that someone would be sympathetic enough to feed us and let us swim in the pool. He's not keen on the idea, and truthfully, neither am I, so we feast on jerky, granola, and drink our water down to the monitored halfway mark.

After twenty minutes of respite we continue uphill and pass another series of buildings I cannot differentiate from offices, storages lockers, and churches. None of them look approachable enough or as if they would sell food or drink or rent a room, which I would overdraft my bank account for at this point. The queasiness kicks in again. I feel like I want to vomit. It's the heat and the probably the McDonald's and the blisters on my feet and the sweat in my eyes. On our right the gates of a cemetery have replaced the rock wall. I tell Saul that I'll hide in the cemetery and sleep until dark if I have to, because it looks safe enough to camp, unlike some of the harrowing neighborhoods we've seen. We walk the span of the gates, about ten yards, and there is a fork in the road where vehicles are completely absent. The cemetery gates have already been locked, and to enter would mean climbing the gates, which we are not quite sure is a good idea. It appears that nobody could be watching us, not a soul, but since we can't be certain we sit under a tree across from the cemetery's sign. It reads 'Grandview Cemetery'. We decide to stretch out, hoping that our bodies need to recharge. Perhaps then we'll be fine to carry on westward.

"I feel like I'm going to die," Saul says.

"I don't know about death, but I do feel a little faint." The shade is like liquid on my hot skin. I stretch out on the ground, rest against my pack, and close my eyes. I look around to take it all in again. There are pines planted in the triangle patch of ground at the fork, all in a row. There are spruces lining the cemetery where we hide from the sun. The grass beneath us has begun to yellow. The sky is blue with thin streaks of white like cursive.

"Maybe we could just stay at this cemetery forever. I don't mind dying here."

"Will you stop talking about dying, Saul? Nobody's dying."

Saul tilts his head and lunges his ear toward the road.

"You hear that?" he asks.

A forest green van pulls over to the shoulder, blaring an old, sad folk song. The woman in the passenger seat waves us in. I can't hear her over the music.

We hop in the back, take off our packs, sit across from each other, and close the door.

"Nice to meet you cool cats," the driver says. "I'm Mike."

"Meg," says the woman in the passenger seat.

"I'm Weston."

"Saul."

"Where are the two of you headed?"

The back of the van is missing any seating, but what it lacks in safety it makes up for in aesthetic value. A clutter of guitar cases, miscellaneous pieces to a drum kit, and vintage posters and album covers lining the walls of the van make this a mobile paradise for Saul.

"As far down 271 as you can take us," I say.

"It just so happens we're headed pretty far down the same road. We'd be happy to take you."

Saul stares at a photo of Johnny Cash on the ceiling. Johnny gazes back down at him like the eyes of God.

"Are you guys in a band?" Saul asks. His hands tremble toward the nearest guitar case. I can only imagine what he would give to pluck just one string.

"Yeah. We're called Infinite Mike and the Pack of Strays. I'm Infinite Mike."

"And I'm the pack of strays," Meg says. They both share a laugh, reaching between the seats to hook each other's fingertips.

"Do you play?" Mike asks.

"Yeah, guitar," Saul answers. He crawls up and sits between the two. "How long you guys been playing?"

While the three of them carry on about music and their different influences, I hang back and check my phone for texts from Lena.

I feel like ur so distant, the most recent one reads. I close my eyes and think of Lena—her eyes so light blue they look like pools of water. The freckles on her nose and cheekbones are little constellations. I've known that I will be her first. I will get back from Pennsylvania and take her virginity.

Do I love her?

I feel Johnny Cash's stern, reluctant visage weighing my sins.

I can't respond to Lena so instead I call my cousin Maggie while Mike, Meg, and Saul chat about whether Jimmy Page or Jimi Hendrix is the best guitarist of all time.

"Is that you, Weston? How are the travels?" On her side of the phone I hear frying pans sizzling and rapid dicing.

"We're about an hour or so outside of Dunbar," I say. "We're with these nice musicians who are taking us the whole way."

"Annie and Fara will pick you up outside the entrance of Ohiopyle," Maggie says. "I hope you're both hungry."

Mike and Meg tell us that Ohiopyle State Park is on the way to their show tonight in Pittsburgh. I really don't know how to thank them enough.

"It means a lot to us," I say from the back. "This ride. Taking us all this way. You saved us at least three days of travel."

"Don't worry about it," Mike says. "Just trying to send out good vibes."

*

We stand on the side of the road and watch as Mike and Meg's van turns around the bend. It is getting dark and the mosquitos have grown fierce. I fear sitting directly under trees to find a tick in my hair, but Saul says that I'm just paranoid. We sit on our packs and talk about how cool Mike and Meg were, and how Saul is so inspired, probably more than ever. He holds an album in his hand, still wrapped in cellophane with a white cover and a green beagle.

"What is that?" I ask.

"A copy of their album. I can't wait to jam out to this."

I get a call from Annie and she tells me she's looking for us, and then I see the headlights of her car illuminate around the bend in the road. Annie and Fara, who is about five, get out and hug us and help throw our packs in the trunk.

"We're so happy to see you," Annie says, squeezing my bicep. "Weston, you got so big since the last time I saw you."

"Thank you for coming out on such short notice," I say.

"Stop all that politeness," Annie says. "Fara, tell cousin West that he's not putting anybody out."

"You're not putting anybody out, cousin West," Fara says, grinning from her car seat.

We're in the car for about twenty minutes and then we pull into the big parking lot that I remember so well. My family's house stands alone and has many parking spaces because attached to the front of a house is a bar called Mt. Lebanon Park, or Zane's Tavern for those in the know, a name that's been carried down the Lebanese side of the family. The parking lot is full, and Annie says that the whole family came out to welcome Saul and me. We enter the side door into the kitchen and the house bellows with familiar voices: Maggie and her other daughter, Autumn—Maggie's older sister, the smoking and gambling nun, Polly—her younger sisters, the twins Riley and Rina and their husbands Pidge and Butch—and all their kids, Ronnie and his wife Junie, Mickey, Jody, Silas, Kath, and Ryan—and all their half-dozen kids. The kitchen is filled with a Lebanese feast prepared by Maggie and her sisters—judra, hummus, grape leaves, kibbe, tabbouleh, baba-ghanouj—and we all eat to our maximum capacity. The food seems never-ending, and we find ourselves in the bar being served Black Russian's by Autumn, and all my cousins are surrounding me, playing their juke and their pinball machine, patting Saul and I on our backs and giving us shots. My soul is on fire, my lungs ripe with laughter. I'm surrounded by faces I haven't seen for years, faces who have only seen mine every five years or so, getting snapshots of me molded through time.

"Drink," Saul says, a beer bottle in one hand, a pool stick in the other. He aims to take a sip of beer from the pool stick.

"I'm giving up on the booze for the night," I say. Already I feel the rum unwillingly bounce my heart to the gut-wrenching sound of Stevie Nicks' voice on the jukebox.

"Your cousins can drink," Saul smiles. "I'm gonna hang out with them."

I look at everyone standing around the bar drinking, eating, dancing—I smile at the fact that my presence is reason enough for them to show such high spirits.

This is the family experience I missed. This is what I needed after my mother died.

"You okay?" Saul asks.

"I think I'm going to go upstairs. There's someone else I'd like to see before bed."

I pat Saul on the shoulder and go walk around the bar and into the kitchen where Maggie sits smoking a cigarette at the table.

"How's the food, kid? You get enough to drink?"

"I'm having a very good time."

"You're drunk," Maggie laughs.

"That I am," I say. I reach for my pack of emergency cigarettes only to find it empty. "Can I have one of yours?"

"They're bad for you," Maggie says, nudging the pack toward me.

I sit down across from her, light a smoke, and look around the kitchen. It used to look so much bigger than it does now.

"You're starting to look like your daddy," she says. "You know my mom's excited to see you. I told her you were coming for a short visit. Don't be surprised if she thinks you're your father." I wonder if she is even truly aware of who I am, even if they did tell her I was coming, because the Alzheimer's renders her memory like a slot machine of nouns.

"Is Aunt Helena awake now? Is it too late to talk to her?"

"She's asleep upstairs. You never know with that woman anymore."

Aunt Helena is my great aunt who lives upstairs in the second story of the house with Autumn who watches over her. I put out the cigarette and follow Maggie up the creaking stairs.

"You'll be sleeping on the couch," she whispers. "It's already been done up with sheets and pillows. The bathroom is down the hall and on the left. And if you need something to drink in the middle of the night the cups are in the cabinet next to the fridge. Make sure you wake up early because I'm making breakfast and I don't want it to get cold."

Once she's out the door I lie back in the dark and stretch out. I feel like I could fall asleep here for the rest of my life. For the next half hour, I imagine one day coming to live here and helping tend the bar.

I start to nod off but instantly wake when my phone buzzes and lights up from a string of Lena's texts.

Why didn't u call me?

I can't wake my great aunt, I type back. She has Alzheimer's.

Oh, she texts. I'm sorry. So when r u coming home?

Saturday, hopefully, I respond.

How r u going to get home?

I swallow hard. That's a good question. Why haven't I thought of this?

I was hoping you'd be able to come and get me.

She sends a frowny face.

I don't know if I can come pick you up. My dad won't let me drive that far.

I don't respond for about five minutes. I just listen to Aunt Helena breathing in the other room.

I can help you pay for a bus ticket back, Lena texts.

I don't even have enough to pay for Saul and I to get back. I've already maxed out my credit card.

For some reason, I feel like Lena's father has nothing to do with it. Maybe she feels like I'm using her.

I thumb through all the texts I haven't replied to on the trip, hoping to find someone who could pick up Saul and me. I consider my roommate, Marv, who dropped us off in Grove City using my car, but he says that it gave him trouble on the way back and doesn't want to risk it again. I consider my father but decide not to because he was so upset with me when I asked him to take over for me cleaning the church so I could take the trip. When my mom died, I lost touch with a lot of people.

As I fall asleep I try to force the thought of ghosts from my dreams.

*

I wake up to the sound of a woman wailing—it's Aunt Helena and it sounds like she's lost in the kitchen again. I listen for Autumn who would be the one to guide Aunt Helena back to her bed, but I wait fifteen minutes and still no sign of her. I can't bear to hear the woman, crying, "Hello? Hello? Jerold? I'm looking for the balcony. I'm locked inside. Jerold? I'm going to pee my pants. Jerold?" There is no balcony, and the Jerold she's referring to would be my deceased grandfather, her brother, who died in a car accident on Christmas when my dad was five, with my father's older brother and Aunt Luna.

I go to the kitchen and see her standing there in her paper-thin nightgown, white hair and saggy skin, trying with all her strength to open the locked kitchen door which has been safety-proofed for her well-being.

"Hey, Aunt Helena, why don't you come back to bed?"

She turns to me, shocked, as if I'm some kind of burglar. "Don't hurt me," she says.

"I'm not going to hurt you, Aunt Helena. It's me, Weston. Zane's son?"

She stares for a moment and then her eyes squint together and she smiles wide.

"Zaney?"

I nod and inch over to her. She takes my hand and says, "Hey, Zaney, do you think we can watch the TV for a bit? My shows are about to start." It's four in the morning and her shows are not about to start, but I guide her to her chair and turn the TV on to some infomercial. She reclines back and smiles so I sit down on the couch next to her. I don't really know what to do or say, so I just watch the infomercial and every few minutes turn to make sure Aunt Helena is still doing good, hoping she will fall asleep.

After a few minutes, I start to doze but jump at her voice asking me, "Have you ever been to Santa Monica, Zaney?" I tell her I haven't, and I don't bother to correct her in believing that

I'm actually my father. She goes on to tell me all about Santa Monica and how she loved the beach when she was a girl, and how she was so angry when she had to move away. Her anger transcends into the moment, and she starts yelling, and I pray for Autumn to run into in the room—but then I see that Aunt Helena has started to pee herself and her screaming just gets louder. I hear the kitchen door burst open and Maggie runs in and tells me not to worry, that this happens all the time with her mother, and to just go back to bed. I go back to the guest couch and try to close my eyes, but I can't fall asleep with the sounds of Maggie cleaning Aunt Helena and scrubbing the chair, and finally singing the woman back to slumber with a soft lullaby in Arabic. I don't know the words or recognize the melody, but I make up my own meaning as I look up past the darkness to the ceiling. I imagine a song of mothers and peace, warmth and angels, and a myriad of roads that lead to here.

Acknowledgments

I would like to thank all the writers, readers, and folks along the way who encouraged me to never stray from the path of writing. Firstly, I would like to thank the late poet, Rane Arroyo, who mentored me to write this story in a different version before his sudden passing (and for teaching how to dance at funerals). Secondly, thank you to Roxana Nastase for considering this story for publication, and all of the other editors who have published my work. For inspiring me to write, thank you to Nicholas Bruno, Alma Luz Villanueva, Jane Bradley and Kyle Minor. For always supporting my work, thank you to Juanita Kniaz, Khalil Carpenter and Megan Aherne. Thank you to Michael Grover, Bob Phillips, John Dorsey, Jim Fahey, and everyone else from the Collingwood

Arts Center. Thank you to everyone from Lunch Ticket, the AULA MFA Program and Library. Thank you to everyone who worked at Barnes & Noble with me and told me to keep writing. Thank you to the friends who stood by me—Chavar Dontae, Nick Liske, Mike Murdock, Paul Spengler, Mark & Krista Dubois, Anne Miller, Brian Clayton, and Ben Maciolek. Thank you to all of the family who took me in, and for your unconditional love. To all my other friends and creative partners, thank you for caring.

And most of all, thank you, Alexi, my wife, for believing in me at all costs. It is all for you.

Author's Bio

NATHAN ELIAS is a writer and filmmaker living in Los Angeles.

His writing has appeared in The Blotter, Red Fez, Hobart, Eclectica Magazine, Literary Orphans, Birdville Magazine and elsewhere.

His films have been selected by Cannes Film Festival, Glass City Film Festival, Texas Independent Film Festival, and other venues.

He has served as fiction, flash prose, art editor, and blogger at the literary journal Lunch Ticket.

This is his first published book. Visit www.TheNathanElias.com for more information about the author.

Thank you for taking the time to read ***A Myriad of Roads That Lead To Here***.

If you enjoyed it, please consider telling your friends or posting a short review. Word of mouth is an author's best friend and much appreciated. Thank you,

Nathan Elias

www.ingramcontent.com/pod-product-compliance
Ingram Content Group UK Ltd.
Pitfield, Milton Keynes, MK11 3LW, UK
UKHW020416250726
13967UKWH00007B/2670

9 781975 786366